Praise for E.J. Stevens
and *From the Shadows*

"E.J. Steven's From the Shadows is lyrical magic that will
bring chills to your spine and a sigh to your soul.
Ms.Stevens paints a vividly haunting picture of love, loss,
joy, sorrow, and a myriad of emotions in between. This is a
collection to be cherished by fans of poetic storytelling,
who aren't afraid of the dark!"
> --Lisa Phillips, author of Obsession Everlasting

"For anyone that loves dark poetry, I think you'll love this
book of poetry written by E.J. Stevens as well....there's
depth to these poems, with a story to be told in each one."
> --Gracen Miller, Moonlight Lace & Mayhem

"With From the Shadows, poetess EJ Stevens has
produced a slim volume thick with dark thoughts and full
of finely wrought imagery....It's a collection of pieces full
of power and humor, and leaves the reader anxious to
follow Stevens back into the shadows for more."
> --Andrew Valentine, author of Bitter Things

"My favorite paranormal poet."
> --Bonnie Lea Elliott, Soul Circle

"Wonderfully, strangely, darkly beautiful with powerful
imagery throughout....the epitome of poetry."
> --Shannon Bailey, Bailey's Books

Also by E.J. Stevens

From the Shadows

Shadows
of
Myth and Legend

By E.J. Stevens

Sacred Oaks Press

Published by Sacred Oaks Press
Sacred Oaks, 221 Sacred Oaks Lane, Wells, Maine 04090

First Printing (trade paperback edition), March 2010

Stevens, E.J.
Shadows of Myth and Legend / E.J. Stevens

Photography by Amanda Stevens
Front Cover Photo Manipulation by Bill Sanborn

ISBN 978-0-9842475-1-6 (trade pbk.)

Printed in the United States of America

PUBLISHER'S NOTE
This is a work of fiction. Names, characters, places, and incidents either are the product of the author's imagination or are used fictitiously, and any resemblance to actual persons, living or dead, business establishments, events, or locales is entirely coincidental.

To my family and friends.
Thank you for always believing.

Contents

Earth & Below

Air & Spirit

Fire & War

Water & Ice

Earth & Below

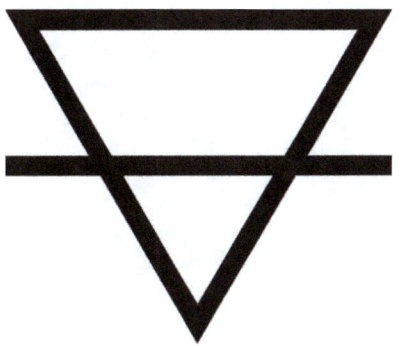

Queen of Elphame

Beautiful Queen of Elphame
Rose wreath garland in her hair
Regal and resplendent
Astride her ivory mare

Radiant sunlight shining
From each silken golden tress
Vibrant green ivy adorns
Her flowing white linen dress

Guardian of cunning folk
Midwives and spirit healers
But woe to those evil men
Pillagers and plant stealers

Those men who dare wreak death here
Who strike down both man and tree
Must do more to please our Queen
Than swear oaths and bend a knee

She will order that they dance
Until they are out of breath
Then command they continue
To suffer a painful death.

Vampire's Thrall

Tracing rivers of blue veins
Encased beneath marble skin
Searching for signs of life that
No longer reside within

Caressing your cheek and brow
Of cold pale alabaster
My sweet one, my life, my love
My dear immortal master

I listen most intently
My head resting on your chest
For a heart that no longer
Beats from deep within your breast

Why did you bind me to you?
How could you make me your Thrall?
My love ran deeper than blood
No need for this curse at all

In life I was so happy
Already under your spell
Making this foul enchantment
Burn with red-hot flames of Hell

Every hour that I live
I am overwhelmed with need
Only you can bring relief
You must come and feed.

Exile

Legs bound with cold iron
So you cannot flee
Wings wrapped in a glamour
For no human eyes to see

Stranded in the mortal realm
No magic to sustain your youth
A terrible price to pay
For seeking out the truth

Exiled from all Sidhe lands
Sent far from kith and kin
Judged by both Seelie courts
Guilty of our greatest sin.

Jiang Shi

Come along now Jiang Shi
It is time to be led
Back to your loving family
To the woman you were wed

You have traveled far from home
Far from your hearth and bed
We must return you to your wife
Whose eyes are rimmed with red

The priest rings the sacred bell
Rice and herbs have been spread
Your flesh is stiff and greenish-pale
Long white hair hangs from your head

We await you in silence
Our prayers have been said
Time to climb into this damp earth
For Jiang Shi you are dead.

Love of a Shifter

Love of a shifter
Changing with the season
Howling at the moon
You would lose all reason

Though I longed to be
Forever by your side
During each full moon
I had to run and hide

Just this once I stayed
Fool curiosity
That which killed the cat
Finally killed me

To stay together
When you emerged as beast
Was my great folly
I have become the feast

With your belly full
Your hunger now sated
So sorry love, I
Never should have waited

Should have kept my vow
To always stay inside
When the moon is full
Birthing your wolf side.

Last of the Rowan Berries

Waxwings have come and gone
Eating the last Rowan berries
Each pale branch now laid bare
None left to ward us from faeries

Each babe in her cradle
Must be checked each morn at first light
To be sure she wasn't swapped
With a Changeling child over night

When the Rowan blossoms
It shall already be too late
For so many mothers
No way to change their bitter fate

Feeding on her sorrow
The child a pale green parasite
Changeling babes suckle life
Leaving their host no strength to fight

Rowan berries ripen
Each bough laden with faerie bane
Babes safe in their cradles
Until the Waxwings come again.

Shadow Queen of the Sidhe

Blackberry lips
Brimstone embers in her hair
The evil temptress beckons
For you to come into her lair

Feet dancing on the dark crags
Legs bare but for swirling mist
She pouts at your indecision
And offers up a kiss

Wrapped in shifting shadows
She sways from side to side
Looks coyly through dark lashes
Opens her mouth wide

A growl escapes her
As she reaches for your face
Shadow Queen of the Sidhe
Wraps you in her dark embrace.

Spriggan Guardians

If you dig for treasure
Hidden under ground
Avoid old sidhe and barrows
Grave and burial mound

A fate far worse than death
For those who dare plunder
The Spriggan guardians
Who ever dwell under

The Spriggan may seem small
But they can swell in size
If someone angers them
And tries to steal their prize

Leave them to their treasure
Which they guard jealously
Or risk that they may grow
To murder you with glee

Tearing you limb from limb
Your shiny eyes they'll save
Adding to their treasure
More souls to share this grave.

While You Lay Sleeping

While you lay sleeping
The small folk seem to hatch
As they all awaken
And climb down from the thatch

For children who are kind
The Brownies do their chores
Working throughout the night
'Till their small hands are sore

But Brownies will punish
Children who tell lies
They steal away their toys
And dump sand in their eyes

The wee brown men believe
That what they do is fair
Punishing the wicked
Tying knots into their hair

To those unkind to pets
They save a special trick
Spoiling each glass of milk
Keeping you weak and sick

Before you go to bed
Do not forget to pray
To become a good child
Protected from the Fae.

Loup Garou

As the last traces of
My humanity recede
Thoughts shift to seeking out
A victim on which to feed

Changing from man to beast
Becoming the Loup Garou
I long to feast on flesh
My next meal may well be you.

Elven Bride

Clans and families gather
In this valley glade with pride
And await the appearance
Of the lovely Elven Bride

Elegance of the high born
Her beauty beyond reproach
Bare foot lightly touching moss
Exiting the bridal coach

Slender legs bring her forward
As all gathered weep and bow
Dancing gracefully forward
Ready for her wedding vow

Clad in a fluttering gown
Of red monarch butterflies
Setting off the sparkle of
Her shining emerald eyes

Alabaster skin gleaming
Her face luminous and pale
Beneath the shimmering threads
Of her spider woven veil

Wet dewdrop diamonds glisten
In her fiery orange hair
Morning sun climbs in the sky
To shine on our maiden fair.

Zombie's Cold Embrace

The nights are dark and empty
Since we laid you in the ground
Darling how could you leave me?
Is it lonely in your mound?

Sleep now but a memory
I lay in our silent bed
Until I hear the scratching
That fills my cold heart with dread

I run to the front window
As you lurch from side to side
You scratch at my unlocked door
I look for a place to hide

From within our closet
Still smelling of your cologne
I peek out to see dead eyes
Staring out of flesh and bone

You grab me with foul hands that
Have begun to rot and spoil
Fingers battered and bloodied
Where you clawed through wood and soil

One final breath escapes me
As you stab me with your knife
Dragging me to your dark grave
Your still warm newly-dead wife

No longer sad and lonely
Deep inside your burial mound
You hold my body to you
My pale lifeless limbs still bound.

Unicorn

Over the maiden's screams
Came a pounding drumming sound
A growing rhythmic beating
Vibrating up through the ground

A flash of brilliant white
As the brigand raised his blade
Fierce, proud, shining Unicorn
Came charging into the glade

He blocked the force of the blade
With his own well muscled chest
Preventing it from plunging
Into the fair maiden's breast

The Unicorn circled back
Nostrils flaring as he ran
Trampling the evil brigand
Leaving no trace of the man

From upon its regal brow
Grew a single spiral horn
So beautiful yet bleeding
Honorable unicorn

The maiden approached him then
Laying her hand on his head
She kissed the Unicorn's cheek
Before blushing brightly red

She sank down to the bare ground
Lifting his head to her lap
He closed his heavy eyelids
Taking one last final nap.

Air & Spirit

Barghest and Mauthe Doog

Barghest and Mauthe
Harbingers of Death
Come to warn this old soul
Of its inevitable last breath

When lightning struck the churchyard
During last night's storm
Red glowing eyes looked out at me
From within a great black hulking form

Your bark became the thunder
Then you were gone into the night
Choosing to heed your warning
I begged the priest for last rites

Today I hear your howling
Echo across the moor
And know I have come at last
To the threshold of death's door

It's time to lay these bones
Deep within the ground
For I have heard, not once but twice,
The baying of the hound.

To See a Fetch

See a Fetch in the morning
Offer it a cup of tea
Live a long life
Of wealth and prosperity

See a Fetch at midday
Walk in a crooked line
Don't catch his eye
Or on your soft flesh he'll dine

See a fetch in the dark night
Hold your friends and loved ones dear
Say your goodbyes
You'll be dead within the year.

Gargoyle Sentry

Faithful gargoyle servant
You ever guard us well
Perched on our cathedral
Beside the tower bell

Dear immortal sentry
Forced to watch forever
Always on full alert
Vigilant as ever

Beneath fearful visage
Lay loyal heart of stone
Left your solemn duty
Eternity all alone.

Siren Song

Your lungs like a bellows
Filled with the breath of the dead
A multitude of feathers
Dancing around your head

Beautiful bird woman
High on your island of death
Where you await male sailors
Who bear life-giving breath

Luring virile sailors
Shipwreck on your rocky shore
Enchanting men with music
They can never ignore

Sweep down with your sisters
Amidst quickly sinking ships
Seeking out the ideal mate
To kiss upon the lips

Drawing in his last breath
Push him under the water
Happy knowing in nine months
You shall bear his daughter

Sun slides below the waves
Day returns to blackest night
The final piece of wreckage
Sinks swiftly out of sight

From atop your aerie
You and your sisters take wing
Moonlight catches ship and sail
You rise once more to sing.

The Reaper

Demons pass outside your window
They call for you
Your hand reaching out to cold glass
Lips have turned blue

Demons dance, leap, twist and gyrate
They never tire
Your hair hangs wet with fever sweat
Eyes lit with fire

Hell's minions gesture and beckon
For your embrace
Trying to stand up, all color
Drains from your face

Promises whispered on the wind
Life without pain
You try to walk to the window
Collapse in vain

Your sobs echo around the room
These prison walls
Demons rally you to get up
With hoots and calls

Demons are tiring of this game
Trace a blood star
You reach out for the window ledge
But it's too far

With chanting and a lightning flash
Demons have left you
All of your hope has gone with them
Wish has come true

Angels now hover over you
To guide your soul
You head for the gates of Heaven
To play your role

You who have known torment will know
Only rapture
Returning to earth with purpose
Souls to capture

At all their bedsides you offer
Blessed release
You take their souls up to Heaven
When their heart's cease

Scythe in hand you do your duty
Take their last breath
With a heart full of righteous fury
Angel of Death.

Warding Charm

Fae folk in the glen
Fae folk by the sea
Fae folk in the sky
Smiling down at me

Magic in the grass
Magic in the trees
Laughter of the Fae
Carried on the breeze

Stars shine in the night
Sun shines in the day
Nothing shines as bright
As the lovely Fae.

Possession

Returning to me once more
Was your dying obsession
When your ghost was strong enough
To attempt possession

You traveled the spirit realm
Seeking the incantation
Finally making a deal
The price your soul's damnation

Yet the demon taught you well
You were right there next to me
But looking into your eyes
Your soul was a raging sea

Your spirit fought for control
Warred with your reluctant host
Struggling to stay corporeal
Terrified to be a ghost

To stay with me you will risk
More than your immortal soul
Giving the coins from your eyes
None left for the boatman's toll

With all your deals and bargains
What no demon would reveal
Was their cruelest intention
Our future they chose to steal

With no way to cross over
Your soul stranded on the shore
When I breathe my final breath
You will be alone once more.

Woman in White

Traveling along the roadside
On this wet fog laden night
I catch a brief glimpse up ahead
Of a lone woman in white

Wondering if I can offer
Assistance to this lady fair
I dismount and call out to her
But she only turns to stare

What foul thing could have befallen
This damsel to strike her mute?
Perhaps then she is no fair lady
But a dame of ill repute

I shall take her with me
I'll keep her warm in my bed
A reward for taking her in
From this road few others tread

Her presence could complicate things
As my wedding night draws near
So long as my wife's family
Remain blind there's naught to fear

A plan already taking form
I reach out to take her arm
But as the clouds move past the moon
Light shines on a wedding charm

Not a harlot then just a bride
Now obvious by her dress
Glowing white beneath the full moon
So lovely but in distress

Trying again to be helpful
I reach out to take her hand
Only then do I see the blood
Dripping onto rock and sand

In her right hand she held a knife
Her left clutched her husband's heart
Her husband had been unfaithful
Tearing her world and mind apart

She looked with frenzied hatred on
A lecherous wretch like me
Quickly slashed head from body
Tossing the head into the sea

So hear me all unfaithful men
Attend these words of the dead
Beware of the Woman in White
Or you too may lose your head.

Fire & War

The Phoenix Cycle

The beautifully plumed Phoenix
Sits upon her aromatic pyre
Beating jewel encrusted wings
To fan flames of purifying fire

As the flames engulf her
She shrieks out a last ecstatic breath
The heat makes her body appear to waver
In this macabre dance of death

Flames burn down to nothing
Red hot embers cool to grey
Night's darkness fades as dawn's light rises
To mark the beginning of a new day

From the ashes she emerges
At first just the appearance of her beak
Shakily rising upward
For as a newborn she is weak

The Phoenix continues pushing forward
Forces open an ash covered eye
Spreads her wings and with a shriek
Launches herself into the sky

As the sun reaches its zenith
The Phoenix gains size and power
But as the shadows lengthen
She must return to her bower

She gathers dry bracken, leaves and twigs
And builds herself a nest
Wondering if this time she will be permitted
The release of final rest.

Fafnir the Wyrm

Greedy Fafnir and Regin
Murdered their loving father
To lay hands upon his gold

Brother set upon brother
Fafnir driving out Regin
Before father had grown cold

Holding tight to his gold pot
Fafnir lay on bloody stones
Face pressed to dirt, grime and mold

He stayed there in the cellar
Beneath his father's castle
Shivering in the damp cold

Coiled around the treasure hoard
Fafnir became a dragon
Better to protect and hold

The treasure he coveted
For his greedy eyes alone
From all men wished to withhold

Meanwhile Regin's jealousy
Compelled him to send his son
Sigurd to Fafnir's stronghold

Sigurd wielded the sword Gram
Killing the dragon Fafnir
With a stroke skillful and bold

Cutting out the dragon's heart
And drinking of its warm blood
Induced the truth to unfold

Sigurd became aware of
His father's murderous deceit
To kill his son for the gold

Sigurd returned to his home
Slay his father and carried
Curse and gold across threshold.

Vampire Court

Ah! The sweet blood of innocents
Always such a lovely vintage
Draining pure young struggling virgins
Conjures a delightful image

My deepest heartfelt gratitude
To our gracious immortal host
For bringing us all together
I would like to offer a toast

To all the long-lived lords and kings
Who linger buried in the dark
Ruling from within the shadows
Each of us prowling like a shark

We will be waiting for the scent
For the peasants to draw first blood
Then we shall strike with combined force
An unstoppable killing flood

We will fill the world with monsters
Brother denizens of the night
Vampires will rule over humans
With pain and paralyzing fright.

Basilisk

King of reptiles and serpents
Murdering all you touch and see
All things burn in your presence
Every flower, bush and tree

Slithering along the ground
Your gaze turns man and beast to stone
Your breath and blood are poison
Turning all men to flesh and bone.

Goblin King

On the horizon marched the horde
Of the Goblin King
Claws smash weapons to shields
Battle drums beating

Our general went to meet their king
On the battlefield
The Goblin King gave
Terms or sword he'd wield

Now if there is but one among you
Not tainted by sin
I will let you all go free
The humans will win

The general agreed to the terms
To avoid slaughter
Goblins and Orcs roared
Filling the air with laughter

Not one among you is free of sin
The Goblin King cheered
Turning to face the humans
His whole army leered

From the direction of the wagons
Came a wailing cry
A woman with newborn babe
Held up to the sky

My child knows nothing of sin
Cried out the woman
Turning the tide of the battle from
Goblin to human

The Goblin King howled and broke his spear
Men! We are not done
You have won this skirmish but
This war is not won

Foul humans I pledge to all your kind
On my broken spear
We will return some day soon
And you shall know fear

The humans turned to the newborn babe
Bowing on one knee
All swore fealty to the man
Who would set them free.

Curse of the Seer

From among the mad
A babe was born
A maiden she shall sing

But this great joy was
Not meant to last
Black tidings she will bring

For when this dear child
Learns to See and
Grows to become a lass

To help aid her friends
She'll scry to see
Evil in the looking glass

In the end she'll look
To see the face
Behind the burial shroud

Wretched oracle
What she sees there
Will make her scream aloud

Looking far beyond
She'll try to learn
The face of the enemy

Seeing past the veil
Finding the truth
By her death will they be free

It was not her fault
But destiny
Her role already foretold

Her friends all vowed then
With heavy hearts
Never to let her grow old

The Dullahan

Dullahan is coming
You cannot bar his passage
Locks fall 'way, gates fly open
At one look from his hideous visage

Fiery hooves striking stone
Cannot flee, nowhere to hide
From the dark cloaked Dullahan
No place his great black horse cannot ride

He holds his head aloft
His neck a bloody wreckage
Darting wide eyes seek you out
To bring his final fateful message

The Dullahan performs
His task with fervor and pride
So do not disturb his work
His rules you must forever abide

Do not look upon him
No peeking from your cottage
Or angry Dullahan will
repay you with bloodshed and carnage

Lashing out with his whip
The spine of a former guide
He'll tear your eyes from your head
Where up until then they did reside

He opens up his mouth
Terrifying grin spread wide
Prepares to call your True Name
Sending your soul to the other side.

Prince of Lies

Our great pious
Benefactor
Works tirelessly
With our Rector

Completing our
Great library
Books set beside
Cinerary

Relics and maps
Sit with statues
All treasure of
Worldly value

This man who brings
Items of worth
He is our guide
While on this earth

So fortunate
Are we brothers
To have him and
One another

The one who brings
Knowledge to us
From far places
Wild and wondrous

Places the book
Upon the shelf
The Prince of Lies
Satan himself.

The Morrigan

Clothed in dark hooded cloaks of crow feathers
Black against the night
Morrigan appear on the battlefield
Causing such a fright
All three raise their arms up to storm filled skies
Drawing deadly might
Eyes roll back as they look at the battle
With prophetic sight
Not happy with the outcome their shriek casts
A green sickly light
Soldiers on one side begin to sicken
With strange plague and blight
More poor soldiers catch the Morrigan's eye
Sword and spear gripped tight
The men turn upon each other killing
All on left and right
Satisfied the Morrigan in a flurry
Of feathers take flight.

Water & Ice

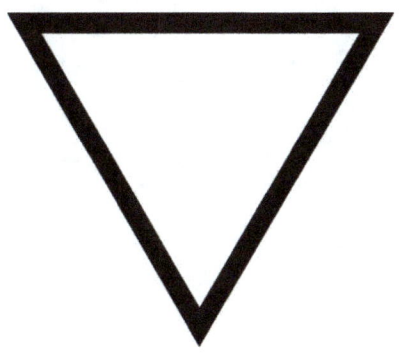

Sating the Selkie

On a splintered and sodden plank
You float upon this misbegotten sea
With bodies floating upon its surface
Like a corpse filled cup of tea

Beneath these depths you dare to dive
Past sirens who do wail
Whilst Selkies feast on the skin stealers
Who in the blackest night set sail

Come to me my love
My tasty morsel of blood and bone
I wish to once again sink my teeth
Though I will end up all alone

Alone alas, yet sated
And that my dear is the catch
I must drink deeply and feed fully
If my little ones are to hatch

Once I bring them forth
Into these dark tumultuous waters
I will no longer be alone
As I swim forth with my daughters.

The Winter Queen

In the dark world of Shadow
During Solstice the Longest Night
The Winter Queen stirs
While her dreaded frost minions
Take flight

In this land of cold and fear
Stands a palace of ice and stone
Where locked deep within
Sits the Winter Queen upon
Her throne

Awareness returns to her
As she tries to open her eyes
Memory and pain
Erupts, but ice seals away
Her cries

The only thing not frozen
Are Winter Queen's immortal tears
Which sparkle as they
Flow down her cheeks mingling with
Her fears

No one dare enter her realm
No man will ever kiss her lips
For death lingers in
Her embrace, into abyss
He'll slip

So on this dark Solstice night
The Winter Queen sits upon her throne
Knowing she will sit here
Forever frozen and all
Alone.

Grindylow

Come hither now my child
Step near the water's edge
There is something waiting for you
Just beyond yonder hedge

Walk just a bit further
Onto the moss slick stones
So the Grindylow may take you
So he may break your bones

Grasping with long fingers
Wrapped around your leg
Grindylow will crack you open
Just like an uncooked egg

He will pull you under
You cannot breathe to scream
He will drag you all the way to
The bottom of the stream

There he will feast upon you
As he dances through weeds
Lost children are what sustain him
Your flesh is all he needs

Unless you now listen
To your old gran this day
And stay far from the water's edge
When you go out to play.

Ghost Ship

Ghost ship on the horizon
Creaking of rigging and mast
Sailing out of fog and mist
Ship sailing out of the past

Seaweed covered rope and wood
Sail cloth rotting and tattered
Faces stare out from the deck
All their hopes and dreams shattered

Eyes full of naught but sorrow
'till they remember the lies
Malice wakens in their hearts
A red glow lights empty eyes

Promised wealth and adventure
They willingly left this shore
Sent into Hell's gaping maw
Cursed to sail forevermore

Left out upon dark waters
Never again to touch land
Reaping souls of men who dare
Walk upon this stretch of sand.

Garden Pixie

There is a Pixie in my garden
Spreading plant seeds and pollen
Nurturing flower and herb blossoms
Though Autumn leaves have fallen

Coaxing seedlings and saplings to sprout
Up through hoar frost covered loam
Waiting for his dearly departed
Dead wife's spirit to come home.

Banshee at Water's Edge

The Banshee wails
As your death draws near
Her keening cry
Emanating fear

Hag of the mist
Goes down to the lake
As twilight nears
Your soul she will take

At water's edge
She pulls forth a shirt
Covered in blood
Not dark stains of dirt

Washing your shirt
The water runs red
Once it runs clear
You will be long dead.

Hippocamp

Little Hippocamp
Stallion of the sea
Poseidon's servant
Never to be free

His chariot glides
High atop the waves
Pronged trident in hand
Pulled by sea horse slaves.

Wendigo

Corpse gray man eater
Denizen of ice and snow
You come down from the dead North
When the arctic windstorms blow

Smelling of decay
You rend with sharp tooth and claw
Forever to wear your curse
You dared break our sacred law

Glutton from the North
During that winter long ago
You murdered and ate your kin
Making your vast hunger grow

Gaunt faced Wendigo
Always hunting your next kill
Hunger cannot be sated
You can never get your fill

Cruel ravenous beast
Feast on human hair and skin
Obsessed with your foul cravings
You commit the gravest sin

Corrupted creature
On blood and entrails you feed
Vile appetites and longings
Damned by your terrible greed

Sick loathsome monster
Gnawing on cold flesh and bone
Forever ruled by hunger
Eternally cast out alone.

Kiss of the Korrigan

Take care brother
As you fetch water from the well
Beware the spiteful Korrigan
Be sure to ring your silver bell

Avert your eyes
If a beautiful maid be there
Singing a lovely ballad
And combing her long golden hair

You must beware
The evil temptress lays in wait
For a naïve man of the cloth
Since we bring out her deepest hate

Plug up your ears
Do not listen as she sings
Her song is imbued with power
Once entranced, death is all she brings

The Korrigan
So like a female praying mantis
She lures to her a foolish mate
Then kills him with her fatal kiss.

Swan Maiden

Take me down to the shore
Where the wild grass grows
We will sit by the marsh
Water lapping our toes
My words may be harsh
Full of hatred and no's

Please dear see through my lies
You're the one for me
Lift me up to the skies
Where all the birds soar free
The wind blurs my eyes
With you I long to be

Come dear save me this day
Change out of this form
Feathers take me away
As swan I'll face this storm
Nothing can make me stay
Feather cloak keep me warm

You brought to me my cloak
Love me forever
Before my captor woke
His head I did sever
Words a gurgling choke
No longer so clever

He thought himself so smart
On that fateful night
My feathered cloak to part
From my body in fright
Forced me in his cart
Beneath the pale moonlight

Beware to all who dare
Approach pond or lake
With splashing maidens fair
For your bones I will break
and rip out your hair
Then your life I will take.

Kraken

Sail across the surface
Shadow against the sky
He will always see you
With his all-seeing eye

Beneath the sea he waits
Kraken the Ocean King
Alert ever watchful
Forever listening

For the heartbeats of men
Who enter his domain
The blight and pestilence
That putrefy and stain

In their vessels of wood
Scurry on his waters
Dumping their poison wastes
Harpooning his daughters

How dare they dump and spill
Barrels of corruption
Always bringing with them
Sorrow and destruction

A realm war has been waged
Blood oaths have been spoken
Peace will be achieved when
All your ships are broken.

The Bestiary

From the Shadows

DARK, DISTURBING, HAUNTINGLY BEAUTIFUL

978-0984247509

www.FromTheShadows.info

About the Author

E.J. Stevens is the author of *From the Shadows* and *Shadows of Myth and Legend.*

E.J. is a graduate of the University of Maine at Farmington with a Bachelor of Arts in Psychology. E.J. Stevens has worked in a variety of jobs that demonstrate the human condition including schools, psychiatric hospitals, and (*shudder*) shopping malls. She currently resides in a magical forest on the coast of Maine where she finds daily inspiration for her writing.

www.ingramcontent.com/pod-product-compliance
Lightning Source LLC
Chambersburg PA
CBHW072233190626
46809CB00017B/1920